StoneSoup

Writing and art by kids, for kids

Editor's Note

This month, I would like to draw your attention to the art by Ashley Jun that you can find both on our cover and throughout the issue. Except for one digitally altered photograph (*Trace*, on page 35), all of Ashley's artworks are abstract watercolors.

Bloom, the cover image, is peaceful and uplifting—the colors remind me of renewal, sunshine, and life. *Monochrome*, on the other hand, which I chose to pair with Meital Fried's excellent, melancholy story "Mourning Dove", captures the way I feel on my worst days: like the world is only black and white. *Waterdrop* also has a melancholy feel, but a softer one than *Monochrome*; it is *blue*, not black and white, and so conveys a feeling of blueness, which is closer to a rainy-day kind of sadness.

Finally, I want to address a question you may have: what do we mean when we call art "abstract"? Abstract art is nonrepresentational, which means it is made of shapes, patterns, and colors rather than images of places, objects, or things. A painting that is obviously "of" something is not abstract. Ashley's painting *Bloom* is not a painting "of" a flower; instead, she has the used title in concert with the colors and shapes to evoke the feeling and idea of the flower.

This month, I challenge you to make some nonrepresentational art—this could mean writing a poem, play, or story that doesn't make "sense," or creating abstract works of art like Ashley.

Till next time,
Emma

On the cover:
Bloom (Watercolor)
Ashley Jun, 13
Short Hills, NJ

Editor in Chief
Emma Wood

Director
William Rubel

Managing Editor
Jane Levi

Design
Joe Ewart

Blog Editor
Caleb Berg

Customer Service
Tayleigh Greene

Special Projects
Sarah Ainsworth

Refugee Project & Book Club
Laura Moran

Interns
Ryan Hudgins, Claire Jiang, Sage Millen, Sim Ling Thee

Stone Soup (ISSN 0094 579X) is published eleven times per year—monthly, with a combined July/August summer issue. Copyright © 2021 by the Children's Art Foundation–Stone Soup Inc., a 501(c)(3) nonprofit organization located in Santa Cruz, California. All rights reserved.

StoneSoup
Contents

Monochrome (Watercolor)
Ashley Jun, 13
Short Hills, NJ

The Mourning Dove

The narrator and her mothers try to come to terms with some terrible news

By Meital Fried, 13
Brooklyn, NY

There was a mourning dove sitting on our roof. Well, sitting might not be the right word. Most of the time, we say one word because a better word doesn't exist. For example, if there was a word that meant *there is a bomb whistling toward your family and all you can do is wait for the explosion which will ruin your life*, then the nurse with purple lipstick would have said it, instead of just "I'm sorry."

And how do you receive an apology when you can never accept it, even if you pretend you can? Most of the time, people act like apologies are gifts the apologizer is giving to the person they're apologizing to. But, looking at the shiny purple lips of the nurse, I wondered what to do with her apology. When you have a gift you don't want, do you still have to write a thank-you note? I guessed you did. So, I just told the nurse, "It's okay." I think that was maybe the first lie in an avalanche of lies. Or maybe it wasn't.

But there was a mourning dove sitting on our roof. And the reason that I wasn't sure that sitting was the right word, is that it wasn't moving at all. Usually when people sit, they fidget, or move their head around if they're a bird. But the mourning dove wasn't moving at all.

"Why won't it move?" asked Aunt Jasmine, trying to pretend everything was normal despite the traces of tears on her cheeks that proved the opposite, looking up at the beautiful bird. It really was beautiful, with its gray-brown feathers with smudges of purple, and eyelids a brilliant blue green. But I didn't want beauty. Or maybe I did.

"Maybe it's *dead*," I said, in a voice that didn't sound or feel like me. The words didn't sound or feel like me, either.

"No, don't, I mean—" Aunt Jasmine's eyes filled with the kind of fear a six-year-old gets. She had flinched when I said the word "dead." "Dead" was the word that the doctors and the nurses had been afraid to say. It disgusted me that Aunt Jasmine was afraid of it too. I wondered if she thought that if we didn't say that word, the bomb wouldn't explode. But it would explode. I knew it would explode. She looked at Aunt Mama.

"It's okay," said Aunt Mama. But we all knew it wasn't. We weren't. *Was that me? The not-okay girl. The not-*

okay family. Aunt Mama was afraid too, only she was trying not to show it, while Aunt Jasmine's fear was too big to contain, so big that Aunt Jasmine had given up trying. She had cried in front of the purple lipstick nurse. But I hadn't. I wasn't ready to give up anything, even with the bomb coming closer and closer. I didn't want to give up. Or maybe I did.

Aunt Mama covered her fear by changing the subject back to the mourning dove, who still hadn't moved.

"You could try to sing to it," she said, acting like the conversation had never changed. Part of me was grateful, but I knew we would still think about the bomb, even when the conversation was elsewhere.

I played a mourning dove's song through my head twice, enough that I felt ready to replicate it. Even with the bomb, we could still have our bird obsession. Aunt Mama and I had always loved birds. Aunt Mama could recognize any bird in the sky, in a bush, or swimming in a lake. I could recognize every bird by their song or call and could respond to them. Aunt Mama called me "The Bird Whisperer," but I really couldn't understand them at all. I couldn't understand anything, really. I couldn't understand why the mourning dove wouldn't move. I couldn't understand why the purple lipstick nurse didn't use a better word, or why a better word didn't exist. I didn't want to understand the words that the doctors and nurses had used, words like "terminal" and "end." Any word but "dead." I didn't want to understand that word either. Mostly, I couldn't understand myself.

So, I tried to sing the song of a mourning dove.

"Coo-oo, coo, coo, coo." The minute the sounds left my mouth, I knew they were wrong. My pitch was too high. Instead of a mournful lament, it sounded like the feeble human imitation it was. I knew how it had to sound in my head, but I just couldn't make it sound right. I tried again twice, but neither was right. One was too low, and one I jumbled up the sounds, even though I usually never jumbled up the sounds. The mourning dove didn't move at all after any of them, didn't even blink. Didn't even sneer, like I would have done if I were a mourning dove.

I tried not to slump, but I think I failed. Aunt Jasmine started to chant "you can do it," but was too exhausted to continue past "you can." Aunt Mama put her arm around Aunt Jasmine and kissed her, but ruined the comforting effect by starting to cry, making Aunt Jasmine cry too. But not me. I didn't cry. The bomb hadn't even exploded yet, and already we were all mourning. But I wasn't going to cry, because I had to be happy before the bomb exploded, even if it was impossible.

Aunt Jasmine and Aunt Mama had sat down on a rock, the big boulder under the oak tree in the backyard. There was room for three people to sit there, but I remained standing. I was too afraid that if I joined them, I would start to cry too. Afraid that somehow the tears would hasten the explosion. I imagined the bomb whistling toward my family. Aunt Mama and Aunt Jasmine were sitting

There was room for three people to sit there, but I remained standing. I was too afraid that if I joined them, I would start to cry too.

on the rock, and I was standing in front of them. I imagined a dark shape falling toward us. The bomb. In my mind, all that existed was the three of us, the rock, and the bomb. There wasn't the sky with dark rain clouds looming above us, or the rest of the backyard or the house. I didn't include the stupid mourning dove either.

The bomb was fast. The bomb was falling. The bomb was coming. The explosion would happen. It would happen soon. And none of us were ready. We would never be ready. The stupid mourning dove didn't know anything about anything. It didn't know about mourning. It didn't know about bombs, or nurses with purple lipstick, or better words for things not existing, or anything. If it knew anything, it should have moved by then. Stupid doves who didn't move at all get killed by hawks and fed to little baby hawks. Hawks that swoop out of the sky like bombs. Bombs that swoop out of the sky and cause purple lipstick apologies. And the mourning dove still didn't move.

Aunt Mama's pale hand was holding Aunt Jasmine's darker one. They were still sitting on the rock. They had both stopped crying, but I knew the tears could and were likely to return at any moment. Aunt Jasmine let go of Aunt Mama's hand and scooched over to make room for me between them on the rock. Without thinking, before I could remember that maybe I didn't want to, I sat down. Even knowing about

the bomb, I felt safe in between my two aunts. Like how small children aren't afraid of monsters when the night-light is on and they are in their warm bed hugging their stuffed bear, even though the monsters are still hiding in the shadows or in the closet or under the bed or whatever. I rested my head on Aunt Mama's large belly. I wondered whose belly I would rest my head on after the explosion. Aunt Jasmine's much smaller belly was always less comfortable. But the warmth of being in between Aunt Jasmine and Aunt Mama pushed it out of my mind.

"Tell me about mourning doves," said Aunt Jasmine, trying to change the subject away from the bomb, even though we weren't even talking about the bomb. Usually if you don't want to talk about something, you end up thinking about it even more than you would have if you had actually mentioned it. But we would have thought about the bomb either way. And if the only subject my aunts could think of to change to was a stupid mourning dove, then the subject would obviously keep slipping back to the bomb the way it had been doing.

Aunt Jasmine was trying to get us to play this game where Aunt Mama and I would tell her facts about a certain type of bird we would be watching. I would tell the stories, what I was best at remembering. Aunt Mama would tell the numbers, which she was better at remembering than I was (she could remember the stories just as well but let me tell them). The idea of doing something so routine comforted me. I snuggled deeper into Aunt Mama and after some thinking, I remembered a fact.

"They eat a lot," I told Aunt Jasmine. "And I think they store it in this place called . . ." I tried to remember, ". . . I think a 'crop,' but I might be mixing that up with another bird." That wouldn't have been the first time that happened. Sometimes bird facts would jumble themselves up in my brain. It mostly happened when I was little, but it had been happening more and more frequently. The bomb had changed everything, even how I remembered bird facts. But Aunt Mama nodded and told me that I was right, so I explained how mourning doves put food they find in their crop, then fly to a safer place to digest it.

Aunt Mama played with my hair. I was hoping she would say how much they eat every day. I couldn't remember the exact number, but I knew she would be able to.

"Aunt Mama, tell us how much they eat every day. Right, they eat a lot?"

"Uh-huh," said Aunt Mama. I could feel her voice vibrating through her belly, where my head still was. Aunt Mama and Aunt Jasmine had this strange way of saying "Uh-huh." Some people, when they say it, mutter it, like it doesn't really matter whether or not someone hears: "Mhm." Some people say it fast, all one syllable, like they're trying to run away from it: "Uhuh." But my aunts had this way of saying it which made it sound like maybe the most beautiful sound on the planet. The "uh" flowed into the "huh," in a way that made the word

sound as important as it was, not trying to run away from the word, not trying to make it feel unimportant, but celebrating it.

Each type of bird has its own unique call, which is for mating, and song, which is territorial. If my family had a call or a song, it would probably have been "uh-huh, uh-huh, uh-huh . . ." Except I couldn't do it. The year before, I had made a New Year's resolution to learn how to say "uh-huh" like that, but I never had. And now the bomb was coming, and it would be too late.

"They eat 12 to 20 percent of their body weight," Aunt Mama said.

I couldn't understand how she could remember so many facts and numbers about birds so well. Of all the things to stick in your brain, who would think that "Mourning doves eat 12 to 20 percent of their body weight every day" would be something you would remember and be able to pull out of your closet of memories on command? A lot of the time, I felt like all of the memories I had forgotten were still somewhere in my mind, I just couldn't find them. Unlike Aunt Mama, I had a pretty bad memory for things like numbers and stuff. I was really only good at remembering bird calls. But Aunt Mama had been a professor of ornithology at Cornell before she had retired two years before, so she *had* to remember those kinds of facts.

I was about to try to think up another mourning dove fact when Aunt Mama's phone rang. I had picked out her ringtone. It was a male gray catbird's song. Gray catbirds are mockingbirds, and a male's song can be a really long and jumbled interpretation of other birds' songs. Aunt Mama's phone didn't really ring very often. Most people knew to call Aunt Jasmine, because she had the better phone, and used it more. Aunt Mama still kept her flip phone because the doctor told her looking at a smartphone screen too much would be bad for her heart or something. But soon it wouldn't matter if she looked at a smartphone screen at all, because the bomb would explode and then all of this time not looking at a smartphone screen wouldn't matter because she would just be the word that nurses and doctors were too afraid to say—dead. They were all afraid of so many words. But I wasn't afraid of words. Or maybe I was.

Aunt Mama gently lifted my head off her stomach and stood up, reaching into her back pocket for her phone. She looked at the caller ID. She looked back at me and Aunt Jasmine, who were both watching her. Aunt Mama looked back down at the caller ID, then again back up at Aunt Jasmine. She mouthed, "Mira". They both looked at me.

"Answer it," said Aunt Jasmine.

Aunt Mama did.

The Woman Who Gave Birth to Me's name was Mira. When she was younger than she should have been, she did the kind of thing that gets you called the kind of names people write on the inside of bathroom stalls. She made the kind of mistake that leaves you with a baby that you don't want. That baby was me. The Woman didn't want me, but she did have a half sister, Aunt Mama, who had just gotten married to Aunt Jasmine, and wanted

kids but couldn't have them with each other because they were gay. So they adopted me. I called Aunt Mama "Aunt Mama" because she was the one related to me by blood, even though really Aunt Jasmine was just as much of a mother.

When I was younger, we had tried to meet up with The Woman once a year to eat ice cream together on the Fourth of July, a holiday that didn't really mean anything to me. I think Aunt Mama had wanted me and The Woman to have some sort of relationship. But over the years, The Woman had started to cancel our ice cream date more and more often. Sometimes she gave a reason, like that she had a date or a friend's party, or she was sick. Sometimes she didn't give any reason at all. When my best friend started hosting a Fourth of July barbecue party, Aunt Mama gave up trying to keep it alive. The truth was, even with the annual meetups, I didn't really know anything about The Woman other than her favorite flavor of ice cream. And now, I was mad at her for calling. I didn't want to deal with anything to do with The Woman now, not with the bomb coming closer and closer with every breath any of us breathed.

The way Aunt Mama's phone worked was that unless you had your ear right next to it, you couldn't understand what the person you were talking to was saying. Still, since Aunt Jasmine and I were nearby, we could hear a high-pitched buzzing sound whenever whoever it was on the other end of the call spoke.

The Woman and Aunt Mama had a short-lived and, from what I could tell,

She might get lonely. Of course she would be lonely. All of us, which wouldn't be complete because it would only be two of us, would be lonely.

fairly unsuccessful attempt at small talk. After a few how-are-yous and all of that, The Woman asked a question, and Aunt Mama looked at me and answered, "Yes, she and my wife are here with me right now." It felt weird for Aunt Mama to call Aunt Jasmine "my wife" instead of "Jasmine." She only called her "my wife" if she was being really formal or was very uncomfortable.

Aunt Jasmine put her arm around my shoulder and squeezed me into her side. Like I said before, Aunt Mama had a lot more cushion than Aunt Jasmine, so it wasn't like an Aunt Mama hug, but it still felt good.

More high-pitched buzzing came out of the phone.

"Just a moment," said Aunt Mama, pulling the phone away from her face and looking up at us. Aunt Mama saying "just a moment" so formally was almost as strange as her referring to Aunt Jasmine as "my wife."

"She wants to be put on speaker," Aunt Mama said.

"Are you up for it?" Aunt Jasmine seemed torn between releasing me and holding me tighter.

"Uh-huh," I said. It didn't sound the way my aunts say it, and it was a lie. Some people just seemed to make me lie. Purple-Lipstick Nurse was one of them, I guess. Another one of them was The Woman, even only the thought of her.

I decided I wasn't going to say "uh-huh" anymore. It just didn't sound right. I thought about how after the explosion, Aunt Jasmine would be the only one left in the whole universe who could say "uh-huh" in that beautiful way. She might get lonely. Of course she would be lonely. All of us, which wouldn't be complete because it would only be two of us, would be lonely. Especially me.

"I'm going to put you on speakerphone," Aunt Mama said after she put the phone back to her mouth. She pressed a button, and then said, "You're on speakerphone now, okay?"

"Uh-huh," said The Woman. The way she said it wasn't the way Aunt Jasmine and Aunt Mama said it, which was good in a way. If she had said it the way they did, it would have made me angry. She wasn't allowed to sound like them. Sounding like my aunts, my real mothers, the ones who actually cared about me, was like saying she was a real mother too. Which she wasn't.

There was a really long silence. No one knew what to say, or had anything they wanted to say, really.

"Hello," The Woman finally said to me. I knew she was talking to me, because she called me by the name on my birth certificate. That name was like her, in that way. It's only real connection to me was through that document. I didn't care about either of them, and neither should really be in my life. But The Woman and the name were both calling, coming at me, and so was the bomb. I was really angry. Usually I wouldn't be that angry, but usually bombs don't fall out of the sky to ruin perfectly nice lives and people who don't care don't come and pretend they do.

"Hi," I said. For the second time that day, my voice sounded like someone else's. Even just saying "hi" to The Woman, I had managed to lie to her, making my voice sound different. But she didn't deserve the truth. She shouldn't have been talking to me. If she didn't care about me before, why was she here now? I didn't need a life that she was in. I didn't need a life that that name was in. Mostly, I didn't want to have a life that the bomb was in. But nobody cared about any of that. I felt tears trying to push themselves through my eyes and out into the world, but I wrestled to keep them back.

"So, I know we haven't really been in touch very much—" I wanted to scream at her but didn't, which for some reason felt like lying too. "But I was thinking that maybe—" she paused for so short it wasn't really a pause at all, and then continued. "Maybe that we could spend some time together over—" Suddenly Aunt Jasmine interrupted her, squeezing me super, super tight.

"She's going through a lot right now, and she's under a ton of stress. I don't think she needs more upsetting stuff in her life right now. You get it?"

I thanked the universe for Aunt Jasmine. She wasn't even formal like Aunt Mama. She just spit it out.

"Oh," said The Woman. "Of course. I didn't mean—no, I understand that it might be upsetting, and I didn't—" The Woman stopped talking and there was a really long, awkward silence. Suddenly and without warning, she hung up.

Aunt Mama put down the phone and looked up at us. First, she looked at Aunt Jasmine. Then she looked at me. Then she looked at the phone, and finally back up at us. There were so many feelings and thoughts in my head, I didn't know what to feel or think first. All of the thoughts and feelings were mushing together into something big, and it was bubbling together, up my throat, fighting to push itself out into the world. I fought back, trying to keep it down. I didn't know what would happen when it came out, and I didn't want to find out. Or maybe I did.

Aunt Jasmine started laughing, and then Aunt Mama joined her. I didn't. All of that laughing was making it harder for me to keep in the bubbling thing that wanted to come out. My aunts laughed and laughed, and I sat there trying to not let all of my feelings fall out of me. I wasn't laughing. It wasn't funny. Besides, right then I didn't want funny. Or maybe I did.

They finally stopped laughing, making it easier for me to hold down whatever it was that wanted to come out. I took a breath that wasn't deep at all to keep it down there. I looked up at the mourning dove, still sitting on the roof. Seeing that it still hadn't moved made me angry.

"It still hasn't moved?" Aunt Mama asked, following my gaze. "Maybe try singing to it again?"

I shook my head. I didn't have the energy. I didn't want to try again. I was tired of failing at everything. I was tired of bad apologies from nurses with purple lipstick. I was tired of words not being good enough. I was tired of stupid mourning doves who didn't move. I was tired of women who decided to come and talk to girls they wished weren't their daughters at the worst time. I was tired of waiting for a bomb to come and ruin my life. And all of my exhaustion was too big to keep in, even though I was too stubborn to let it out.

Aunt Mama went in to make dinner, and I wondered who would make dinner once the bomb exploded. Aunt Jasmine was a notoriously bad cook. Maybe we would just order pizza every night. But I didn't think that even eating pizza every night would make up for everything the explosion would take away from us. A million nights of pizza could never, ever, replace Aunt Mama. Aunt Jasmine put her arm around me, but this time didn't squeeze so hard.

"Tell me more about mourning doves," she told me.

I didn't want to. I really didn't want to. Why did I have to? Aunt Mama could tell Aunt Jasmine a million bird facts with no effort, any time she wanted. But not any time. She wouldn't be able to after the explosion. I felt Aunt Jasmine's arm around me. It was kind of loose, in a dejected sort of way. But it was still around me. And I remembered how afraid she had looked when I said the word "dead." Remembered how she had spoken to The Woman. And then I knew that Aunt Jasmine *needed* me to tell her a fact about mourning doves. So, I tried to remember.

"The oldest known mourning dove lived to be pretty old," I finally told her.

"How old?" she asked, squeezing

me. I knew she was glad that I had played along.

"I can't remember!" I said. My voice broke. For the first time that day, something I said felt true, and not like a lie. My broken voice was like me. I was broken too.

It started to rain, so we had to go inside. I would have stayed out there, in the rain, but I was too tired to say so to Aunt Jasmine, and I didn't think she would have listened to me either way. I was glad it was raining, so I got to pretend that my tears weren't rolling down my face, and not hate myself for them. The stupid mourning dove was still sitting there, on the roof, in the rain, not moving a muscle. It was drenched. It deserved to be. I don't know why I blamed everything on it, but it felt good to have someone to be angry with who wasn't me. Before I went inside, I looked up at it.

Aunt Jasmine had already gone inside, so it was just me and the bird. Looking at it, all of my feelings bubbled up in me again, but this time I could recognize them better. Anger at The Woman. Anger at myself. Anger at the mourning dove. Anger at the bomb, and whatever sent it. Grief. Fear of the grief. Fear of forgetting everything important. Anger at myself for being the kind of person who might forget. All of that, and all of this other stuff that I still can't explain, clumped together into this big, explosive thing inside of my chest. And I focused all of it at the mourning dove. It all came up and out of me like a storm, like a bomb, like an explosion, like a falcon swooping down to eat stupid mourning doves who didn't move. And I screamed at

And I screamed at the mourning dove. But it wasn't a scream. It was small. It was quiet. It was hollow. It was everything I was at that moment. And the funny thing was, it sounded exactly like the cry of a mourning dove.

the mourning dove. But it wasn't a scream. It was small. It was quiet. It was hollow. It was everything I was at that moment. And the funny thing was, it sounded exactly like the cry of a mourning dove.

The mourning dove turned its head and looked at me. Usually it's hard to read a bird's face and see what emotions are in it, because bird faces are so different from human faces. But right then, I could see everything I needed to in the mourning dove's eyes. I could never explain what I saw there to anyone. I think even if I could, they wouldn't understand it. But I understood it. It was one of those things you don't need words for. Words hardly ever do their job. Sometimes all you can do is *feel*. And I felt. Then, the mourning dove spread its wings, and flew away, leaving me alone, all by myself. I turned around and walked into the house.

———————————————

After dinner, and once the rain had slowed a little, the three of us put on our raincoats and went back outside to see if the mourning dove was still there. I hadn't told my aunts that it wasn't. But when we went outside, it was still gone.

"I guess it went someplace dry," said Aunt Jasmine. "Birds do that, right?"

"Uh-huh." Aunt Mama said it in that beautiful way, but I wasn't jealous anymore. "That's one of the benefits of nests. They provide some shelter against weather."

We were all quiet for a while. My head was resting on Aunt Mama's belly, like before, only now we were both wearing raincoats, so it was a little less comfortable. I wished I could freeze time forever in this moment. I wished the rest of my life would be this comforting, and not stressful or confusing or uncomfortable or upsetting, like so much of life is. I tried to memorize everything about the situation, so I would still have the memory even after the explosion.

"Are you . . . scared?" I asked Aunt Mama. I didn't have to explain what I meant. I didn't know if she thought about her sickness as a bomb the way I did, or maybe something else. Maybe she just thought of it as a sickness. Maybe she could pronounce the long, complicated name that the doctors had called it. She didn't say "scared of what?" or lie that she wasn't scared. She just said, "Yes."

She didn't say her beautiful "uh-huh." I didn't think it fit there, and I guess she agreed. I had known she was scared. I had seen it when I had said the word "dead," the same way I had seen it on Aunt Jasmine's face. I just needed to be reassured that I wasn't the only one.

"I'm sorry about all of this," she said after a while. Earlier I might have blamed her a little, but if I did before, I didn't then. Her apology wasn't a purple lipstick apology. It wasn't what it was because something better didn't exist. It was what it was because it needed to be. I knew what to do with it too. I knew how to respond. And I didn't lie.

"It's not your fault," I said. And I wasn't just talking to her. I was talking to myself. I was talking to the purple lipstick nurse. I was talking to the mourning dove. I was talking to Aunt Jasmine too, who probably blamed herself a little bit the way I had. It wasn't anyone's fault. Sometimes sad things just happened.

"Are you scared?" Aunt Mama asked me.

"I am," I said. I burrowed deeper into her belly.

"I am too," Aunt Jasmine interrupted, suddenly. "But you know what?"

"What?" I asked.

"We're gonna figure it out," said Aunt Jasmine. I could feel her lean over and put her arm around Aunt Mama. And there we were. My beautiful family. It was only drizzling a little now, and the horizon was starting to get orange with the very beginnings of sunset. But the sunset didn't remind me of the bomb by the way it was looming. It only made me think about sunsets. I wondered if we would see a rainbow, but the only time I had ever seen a rainbow was in a hose, which I didn't think counted. And it didn't matter if the sunset wasn't beautiful at all, or if there wasn't any rainbow. I think we were beautiful enough.

"Uh-huh," I said, and it sounded exactly right.

A Beautiful Abundance of Birds (Acrylic)
Sophia Swanson, 11
Novato, CA

Two Poems

By Emma Catherine Hoff, 8
Bronx, New York

How to Share an Apricot

I shared
My apricot
With a bird.

It said,
"Thank you."
I don't know when the bird started talking.

It wrapped me in its arms.
It had a gentle grip.
Such a gentle grip.
Too gentle of a grip, I thought.
Supernatural.

I don't know
When the bird grew arms.

All I know
Are my thoughts.
Right then I was thinking this was not a good way to show gratitude.

I didn't know
Where it was taking me.

But then the bird vanished.
Its gentle grip was gone.
And I was falling.

I landed
In a queer place.
Above me
Stood a human with a beak.

And I knew at once
That it was Carry,
The animal I shared my apricot with.

All I could think was the
Sweet, sweet fact
That above me there were several apricots.

And I wanted to have one.
For I had shared mine earlier today
With a bird.

Dear Friend

They are dressed as if they just went to a funeral.
Which they have.
But only I know.

They went to mourn
In Los Angeles,
And are staying at a hotel now.
They are probably taking off
Dresses and ties.

They're coming home tomorrow.
I begged to go
But Mom asked me what funeral I was talking about.

Yesterday
I got a letter.
It said,

"Dear friend,
We miss you.
We are coming home soon.
The funeral was sad.
Wish you could be there.
Love,
Your friends."

Today
My friends
Came back.

While I helped them
Take off their coats,
One of them asked,
"Did you get our letter?"

I felt happy
Even though the handwriting on the letter
Was mine.

Looking Up (iPhone 6)
Anna Weinberg, 11
Washington, DC

The Day the Sky was Orange

"When will our world go back to normal?" the narrator wondered, as smoke blanketed the California sky during the pandemic

By Raya Ilieva, 10
Belmont, CA

I knew something was wrong when I saw bright orange light peeking through the cracks in my blinds. Quietly, I slipped out of bed and opened one shutter. What I saw was appalling: a yucky yellow hue tainting everything outside.

The world outside is cloaked in a haze, yellowish-orange in color. The sun is completely obscured by the thick substance, giving off minimal light and making our whole world dimmer than normal.

I'd heard stories from my classmates about the yellow sky that was outside their homes, with a bright orange sun suspended in it. One of my best friends, with whom I had a Google Doc in the times of quarantine, put a photo there of the exact thing that my classmates were describing. *It can't be true*, I thought. *These fires are so far away—how can the smoke drift all the way over here? And obscure the sun? Impossible.* And then it happened to us.

It's a little bit past noon now. The sky has passed its yellow phase—now it's a deep orange, the color of a ripe pumpkin. It's as if giant streetlights are shining on us from the sky, flooding California in amber light.

It's actually not all smoke. There's some fog too. But the smoke is high up and is ultimately what is covering the sun, filtering out all but the orange light.

The mountains, usually so proud and defined, have blurred and softened edges. Their color is unclear, a hazy greenish-gray. Through the orange sky, sweeps of gray smoke smudge it.

Our hummingbirds are going crazy. Just today, they've drunk at least two feeders' worth of sugar water. Maybe more. While normally we would be able to see their beautiful red throats and iridescent green backs, now they are simply dark silhouettes flitting in and out of the eaves of our deck.

As I stare out the window at the pumpkin-colored expanse outside, I wonder the same something that I've wondered for a while now: *when will our world go back to normal?*

Please let it be soon, I think, and go back to staring at the surreal orange sky.

The Secret Society

Twenty years in the future, an orphan boy tries to find his place in a world permanently altered by COVID-19

By Chloe Leng, 12
Hinckley, Ohio

The boy dragged his metal wagon down the crumbled pavement.

Thump, thump, thump. The cart wobbled every time it hit a piece of loose asphalt. Each package in it was wrapped securely in plastic to keep the contents from sliding out during the unstable journey. Each week, the boy distributed such parcels, often to the rich.

Pulling the wagon to a stop at his next destination, the boy rapped on the metal structure at the edge of the road. The structure had lines splitting it into thirty boxes. Immediately, the small camera installed on the top of the structure swiveled down to look at the boy, and after a minute, the boxes swung open.

He took out his list, which had names and numbers, then stuffed the packages into their corresponding boxes. He repeated these actions at each stop until the wagon was empty.

When the boy reached his city, he saw people milling around: shopkeepers, shoppers, and a few security guards to make sure everyone was wearing their mask and that they were at least six feet apart to avoid infection from close contact. There were guidelines along the sidewalks and on posters to keep everyone "distanced and safe."

The boy hauled the wagon to a large building. This building was owned by the government, his employer. He left the wagon at the entrance to be refilled with packages for the next day. These packages were from all over the world. Sometimes, the packages clinked with toys or shifted with clothes from China. Other times, rich scents wafted from the packages, like cinnamon from Sri Lanka or coffee from Colombia.

Strolling down the smooth, paved city streets, the boy glanced at the shops that he passed. Every shop had notices tacked to its wooden doors. One said, "No mask? No entry!" Another read "Limit of 4 persons."

As he walked, the boy thought of the thing that had brought him into this situation. COVID-19, named after the year it had first infected the human race, was a virus that had never stopped terrorizing the world. Ever since he could remember, the cardinal rule was to wear his mask everywhere. As time passed, social-

A Divided World (Colored pencil)
Sabrina Lu, 12
Ashburn, VA

distancing guidelines became more strict. People started avoiding going out until certain times in the day, and they slowly fell into a routine. A curfew was enforced to make sure nobody snuck out of their homes to meet secretly. There was also a time limit for how long the boy was allowed to spend on deliveries. He had to be back at a certain time and couldn't leave the city after that.

The boy was born in 2026, a year after the Split happened. The Split was a plan, contrived by Congress, to separate the rich and the poor. As the pandemic had grown worse, tensions had risen between the middle and lower classes over race, politics, medical care, and money. The elite sat idly by, watching with contented smiles as their "inferiors" tore each other apart. They felt no need to help them.

The boy was lucky he wasn't alive during those fights. He had heard about how gruesome they were. His parents probably had had to face that, but it didn't matter: they were dead now anyway. He had never met them and only knew the orphanage in which he grew up. Because of his low status, he had ended up in an unimportant city and was essentially stuck at the bottom of the societal food chain.

The boy had no significance, so he was given the menial job of delivering goods to close cities. Since no one else could work with the boy because of safety regulations, he was always isolated, day and night, with no friends or even acquaintances.

The next day found the boy up and running before the sun.

After dropping off the packages, the boy delivered his wagon back to his city and left to take his evening stroll.

The city sat by the edge of a forest that eventually gave way to a highway. No one used it anymore, save for the occasional little critter. The boy had always wondered what was on the other side, but he had never had the courage to break the rules and leave the city unless it was for his job. But now he was in his adolescent years, reaching a state of rebellious attitude and independence.

When the boy crossed the highway, he could see an old city that had been abandoned. That city had once been populated by rich businessmen and their families, who would travel there to their winter or summer homes. They had been transported to safer cities during the Split.

Amidst the buildings on the outskirts of the city was a large box with opening on one side. It led to a series of steps. The boy descended the steps carefully. He did not realize how deep underground he was until he became aware of the chilliness and wetness of his surroundings.

The passage the boy was walking along had flickering lights that hung from the high ceiling. Everything, including the walls and the graffiti on them, looked old.

The boy didn't know how long he had been walking through various winding passages when he began to hear voices. They sounded different than the occasional voice he would hear in the city, although he couldn't

Everyone was touching—holding hands, knees knocking together when they moved, elbows bumping, backs pressed against each other. No masks.

place what made them so different. Curious about why people were out this far from a city, the boy decided to investigate.

As he walked down a final set of stairs, the space around him opened up into a big room. There were tunnels on both the far right and left sides of the room. Tracks that looked much like the railroad tracks that the boy sometimes had to cross while he was working were laid down at the bottom. Long strips of lights were attached above the tunnels.

Although the boy saw this, his attention was immediately drawn toward the people sitting on a set of stairs on the opposite side of the room.

Here was the boy's analysis of the odd group: Everyone was touching—holding hands, knees knocking together when they moved, elbows bumping, backs pressed against each other. No masks.

They obviously opposed the Split. The boy remembered hearing a bit about this group before. He dimly recalled hearing about riots and protests from a group of people the president had dubbed "Peacebreakers." They were given this name to symbolize them as outcasts to the public and to show that they were destroying the peace that the Split brought. They weren't rich or poor, but a mix of both who shared a common belief: to oppose the Split and show that life would be better if humans stuck together.

At the beginning of the Split, the Peacebreakers had stayed hidden, to protect themselves from prejudice and malicious actions and comments. Now as people thought less of others and more of their own safety, the Peacebreakers were left alone. Although they did not matter anymore to anyone, they could not expose themselves to a world they knew nothing of. They would be vulnerable to more attacks if they were rediscovered.

Something inside the boy felt elated that he had discovered this population. An unprecedented way of living, an unexpected harmony among people.

The boy was curious, but also frightened. Instead of protective masks or face shields, the boy saw wrinkled and young faces alike. The noses and mouths that were twitching and moving scared him.

"Hello, boy. Who are you? Where do you come from?" an old man rumbled.

As the man opened his mouth to speak, the boy imagined large green particles in his spittle flying across the room, their dangerous red protein spikes reaching for a place to infect him.

He moved his mouth, but no sound came out. His face flushed a bright red that was mostly covered by his mask. He was overwhelmed by his senses. First, the voices. Then, the smell of mildew and rotting garbage. Then, the blinding lights.

By now, everyone had stood up, and there was only about three feet between them and the boy. This was less than the boy was comfortable with, but the crowd kept pushing forward.

I'm gonna suffocate. I'm gonna drown among bodies. Lonely, but not alone, the boy thought. Among strangers, he would die. A new world discovered, only to be trampled.

The boy squeezed his eyes shut but didn't feel a wave of crashing limbs. Instead, when he opened his eyes, he saw curiosity on the people's faces. It was like they had never seen another person before.

Although nobody took another step forward, the old man extended his hand.

What is this? The boy mirrored the man's gesture and looked oddly at his own hand. Chuckling, the old man said, "It's a greeting, son. Shake my hand."

Instead, the boy shook his head. The old man's smile faltered. He looked disappointed, but understood the boy's discomfort.

Though the boy felt wary, he also felt like these people accepted him like one of their own. It was against his nature and everything he had been taught to be mingling with these strangers, but the boy felt a connection and that somehow he had to help them and learn about their movement.

After refusing the old man's greeting, the boy nodded his head and took off without a second thought. He only stopped running when he reached the box-like structure. He looked down into the darkness and stood confused for a while. *What did this all mean? Why did it matter? What was he going to do about it?*

On his way back to his city, the boy hesitantly took off his mask for the first time outside of his home. With no one around, the boy breathed in the cool air and felt it fill his lungs in a way masks would not allow. He felt refreshed. *This must be how the Peacebreakers feel all the time, he thought. How wonderful . . .*

That night, as the boy lay in his bed, he peeked at the mask that he had thrown on his table. *Was it really necessary to keep everyone safe, or was it just a useless precaution?* After all, the boy had seen the consequence of taking off a mask and it wasn't at all as he had imagined.

After his next day of work, the boy stood on the edge of the highway. From this far away he could not see the Peacebreakers' lair, but he knew it was there. A little smile could be seen on his uncovered face. His mask lay a few feet behind him, completely forgotten.

Even though his visit underground had been short, he felt a renewed energy, with the hope that he might one day be reunited with this newly discovered secret society.

My Eyes Stretch

By Avery Lakomy, 12
Chicago, IL

North, south, east, west
My eyes stretch into different directions
Regions are divided before my eyes
Separate places I'm taught

But my compass rose must be broken
All I can see is one region
Aren't we all living together
Instead of being separated by the paths of the wind
Or by all the people of the regions

Why can't we all fit into one place
Where we'll accept each face
No one will win
No one will lose
No one will even have to choose over people

What region am I in now

Love Sculpture (Wire, electroluminescent wire, wood)
Penny Gottesman, 10
Arlington, MA

Gentle Hands

It's Michelle's first day of school, and all she wants is to be in bed at home, with the familiar sound of Chinese filling the air

By Michelle Wang, 12
Lexington, MA

All I could see was the dark blue carpet beneath my feet, blurring and clearing as I held back the tears in my eyes. My hand, cold and frail from the lashing winds outside, latched on tightly to the corner of my mom's winter jacket, afraid to let go. I dug my nails into the soft, velvety fabric so hard I was afraid it was going to rip into shreds. I felt the stitches, one by one, as I pressed my other hand down deep in my pocket. My eyes stung, as if someone had squirted fresh lemon juice straight into them, as I barely managed to hold back my tears from pouring out like an endless waterfall. I just wanted to go home. I wanted to go back to the comfort of my bed awaiting me and welcoming me into its affectionate arms. I wanted to go home, where someone, anyone, would wrap their strong arms around me as they comforted me and told me that everything was going to be fine. Suddenly, a woman walked into the room and bent down to me.

"Hi! Welcome to first grade! I'm your teacher, Ms. Muzyka," she greeted me cheerfully. "Can you understand me?" she asked, speaking slowly.

I turned my head slightly and stared back at the bare ground. She was unlike any teacher I had ever seen before, with her chocolate-colored brown hair and bright caramel highlights. She had big round eyes, the color of the sky on a bright summer day. Her smile was so sweet and sincere, it felt misleading. Maybe it was like a needle inside a chocolate bar, gaining your trust, then stabbing you right back. Maybe seconds later, she would jump into reprimanding and screaming at me, like most teachers I'd had. But this time, I could not convince myself to believe so. I wished she could just flash out the mean side all teachers are supposed to have and scold and yell in the way I was used to, but she didn't.

To my surprise, she took me by the hand and led me across the room. Her hands were warm and soft, like freshly washed towels, cradling me in warmness. She dragged me to the opposite corner of the room, where the floor was lined with a rug filled with all the colors of the rainbow. There were baskets of stuffed animals with black beady eyes and soft bodies sitting by a shelf of books. On the walls were pictures of characters, from colorful, spiky dinosaurs to striped cats wearing giant red hats.

I trotted toward the shelves of books to see even more characters woven between letters and words I could not make sense of. When I glanced at the windows, I saw messy drawings of all kinds of people. Some with black eyes and brown hair like me, others with strawberry-blonde hair and rosy red lips. Nothing seemed familiar. I glanced back down at the floor as I felt another tear roll slowly down my cheeks. The bright colors of the rugs seemed to have lost their luminous glow, and I descended into a world of darkness.

"I'm sure she'll do just fine," the teacher reassured my mom, followed by another perfect smile.

No! I will not be fine, I thought stubbornly. All I wanted to do was go back home. Home, where I could understand everything and everyone. Home, where the familiar sounds of Chinese rang happily in the air. Home, where everything is all settled. Another unintentional tear rolled slowly and heavily down my cheek.

Suddenly, the back door opened and I was hit with a wave of the cold, winter air, sending chills down my arms. The sound of ripping Velcro boots and shrieks and laughter filled the room. There was the loud chatter of words, some I could not wrap my head around. I felt the whooshing air pass by my ears whenever someone walked past me. I could feel the eyes staring and burning straight into my skin. I quickly looked at the ground and slouched into my winter coat, my face flushed red with embarrassment.

Then, I felt a gentle tap on my shoulder. I turned my head around nervously to see a girl with bright-red cheeks and a pink, fluffy sweater. She had straight, dark hair and light brown eyes like marbles, glistening with every look.

She smiled at me and asked, "What's your name?"

"Mi-Michelle," I replied with a tremble in my voice as I wiped the last tear off my face.

"Do you wanna come play with us?" she asked, eyes filled with curiosity as she pointed toward another group of kids sitting by the bookshelf. I slowly but surely nodded my head as she pulled me away.

Strangely, I felt warm as her icy cold, yet gentle, hands latched onto mine. A feeling of comfort and happiness surrounded me, as if I had just opened a pot of freshly steamed rice. I glanced back at my mother and she smiled at me. It was almost as if she was saying, "I believe in you." I watched her step confidently out of the door, her eyes glittering with hope, as I managed to squeeze out a slight smile and sat down with the others.

Name

By Tessa Hsieh Schumacher, 10
Los Angeles, CA

Tessa sounds like clear blue streams, as the water flows peacefully
     and silently away,
Like a piece of sheet music just lying there, waiting for someone to finally play.
It sounds like an echo through the mountaintops,
Or a beautiful dress sitting in the shop.
Like the soft flutter of a butterfly's wings,
As the young girl reads and the sparrow sings.
It is a shy tiger waiting to roar—
My name is always there, deep inside my core.
Tessa is the base, the courage in me,
Venturing through life and seeing the trees.
Tessa is unique and special and my own,
It is a beautiful artifact. It is my gemstone.

The Blue Below (Canon PowerShot SX600 HS)
Sage Millen, 13
Vancouver, British Columbia, Canada

China is Left Behind

By Alisa Zou, 12
Concord, MA

I can't stop myself
From looking out there.
Like something is
Controlling my eyes,
Pulling my head towards
The airplane window
Again and again
Seeing America
Below us.

Ladies and gentlemen,
Please go back to your seats and
Fasten your safety belts.
Thank you.

Tears suddenly
Race out of my eyes like a lake across my face.
I can't stand it!
China is now
A long way left behind.

Mom!
I want to
Go back now!
I cry.

I Wish . . .

A mother and a son, separately regretting the way they've treated each other in the past, wish to make things right

By Michelle Byers, 13
Bellevue, WA

March 20, 2020: "When I talk about the most drastic action we can take, this is it. New York is locked down; New Yorkers will only be allowed to leave their homes for essential business."

Diana sighed and switched off the radio just before—

"Mooom? Can you come in here for a second?"

Will's mother sighed as she rose from the worn wooden chair in their kitchen, leaving a pile of bills scattered on the table. She walked down their apartment's short hallway, stretching stiff limbs long overdue for movement, and stopped outside Will's door. She closed her tired eyes, swept back her unbrushed hair, and smiled.

"What do you need, sweetie?"

"Uhh, we're supposed to be analyzing this book we read . . ." Will clenched and unclenched his fists nervously, "and the essay's due tomorrow . . ."

Will's mom inhaled sharply and rubbed her forehead, "Will, what did I tell you about your homework?" She pushed her hair back in distress. "Look, I just don't have time right now, hon . . ."

"Alright, fine. Fine, I get it," Will interrupted and muttered, "I don't need you anyway."

Will's mom glanced up in surprise. "You know I don't mean it that way . . ."

"I don't need you, Mom! Just"—he sighed—"just get out!"

Will's mom stood frozen, hurt. She sighed and shook her head as she backed out of his room.

She plopped back into the creaky wooden chair in their kitchen and let her head fall into her hands. A tingling sensation moved down her right arm and she looked at her copper bracelet. She smiled, fondly but sadly, remembering her mom who had given her the bracelet decades ago. She could barely believe a woman of such strength and happiness had been taken by the virus. No matter what, her mom had always been there for her, and she aspired to be that for Will. Will!

Quiet terror swept across her face as Diana remembered all the times she had put Will's needs on the backburner. *I wish . . . I could just go back and redo everything . . .* Diana sighed. *I just want to go back to when he was born and be there for him.*

Trace (iPhone XR, Adobe Photoshop)
Ashley Jun, 13
Short Hills, NJ

Suddenly, she felt the copper bracelet on her arm slowly beginning to turn counterclockwise. It was barely moving at first, but it spun faster and faster. From the window of her fifth-story apartment, she watched in shock as the days began to pass in more and more rapid succession. No. The days . . . they were rewinding!

Will shifted in his chair and smiled smugly. *Ha. I finished my essay, and I didn't even need her*, he thought defiantly.

"Mooom," he called as he finally rose from his chair and wandered into the kitchen.

He was met with silence and an empty room.

"Mom?!" he called out louder.

Will jogged back down the hallway and swung into his mom's bedroom. *Hmm. She's not here either*, he thought nonchalantly. He walked across her room and found the bathroom dark and empty. *Weird*, he thought. *She must be around here somewhere. I didn't hear her leave . . .*

"Mom?" he called out again.

Will's face began to contort with worry, and then frustration. *I didn't really mean what I said before about not needing her*, he thought. *She knows that, right?*

Will pushed his hands through his hair, lifted his right foot, and stamped it down with all his weight. Suddenly he caught sight of the kitchen phone. *How could I be so stupid?*

He snatched the phone from the wall and punched in his mom's phone number. The flip phone amidst a scattering of bills rang abruptly. His hope vanished, and a tear splashed quietly onto the tile floor. He solemnly made his way to his mom's bedroom and opened the top drawer of her dresser, pulling out a small jewelry box. Inside was a thin bracelet of tiny copper chains. It was one of two matching bracelets Will's grandma had handed down to his mom. His mom had tried to offer it to him, but like always, he had met her question with an unnecessary amount of aggression and opposition. Now he gently lifted the bracelet out and clasped it around his wrist.

"I wish this would just be over already," he whispered in a subdued sob.

The copper bracelet began to rotate around his wrist clockwise. It circled faster, faster. The view outside the bedroom window blurred into a confusing mixture of night and day, until the sun stopped and hung bright and still in the sky.

Will stepped out of his apartment building and looked around at the streets in frantic confusion. He jogged along the sidewalk and called out, "Mom?!" The people around him glared judgmentally before hurrying on their way. Will was still apprehensive to move about without a mask on and in such proximity to other people. But no one else seemed to share his concerns.

"Ma'am? Isn't New York City on lockdown to prevent the spread of COVID-19?"

"Two years ago, we were," she replied, bemused.

Will furrowed his brow. "Two years ago?" he repeated quietly to himself.

He wandered into the Apple Store across from his apartment building, still pondering the reply. Buried in thought, Will felt himself hit the hard, cold frame of a metal shelf. Startled, he looked up and muttered angrily at the shelf. Then his eye caught the large display on the nearest wall showing an ad for the iPhone 14: scheduled release—September 2022.

Will quickly walked over to the nearest employee. "Excuse me. Are you sure that release date's right?"

"Yep, it's right. Just a month away!"

Will rushed over to the phones and tablets on display. They all read August 12, 2022. He ran outside, panicking. The employee watched him and shrugged as he turned to another customer.

Will needed to get to back to 2020, back to his apartment, and most importantly, back to his mom. But he had no idea how.

Diana stumbled back in confusion, reaching for the flip phone that was usually safely stowed in her back pocket. She winced, remembering her flip phone still lying on her kitchen table. Dust caught in her throat, and she coughed. To her surprise, no one backed away in worry from the short, black-haired woman who had just coughed. She took a deep breath and let the confusion melt from her face. Gathering herself, she stopped a young man walking toward her.

"Hi, sorry. Do you happen to know what today's date is?"

"November 2," he answered.

"Wait, what?" Diana whispered under her breath; it had just been March . . .

"Yeah, November 21, 2003." The young man held out his Blackberry displaying the same date.

Diana suddenly realized something particularly odd about the date, besides the fact that it was nearly two decades in her past: it was Will's birthday!

"Is it a coincidence? Why am I suddenly here on Will's *birth*day . . .?" She slowed to a stop and let the crowd flow around her. Tentatively, she inspected the copper bracelet on her wrist. "Is it possible? My wish . . . came true?"

Diana was quickly snapped out of her thoughts as she came to the harsh realization that she wasn't pregnant. "But then who's having my baby today?" she whispered.

Jogging to the edge of the street, she held out her arm. "Taxi!"

She threw open the yellow door and hurried inside.

"Where to today, ma'am?"

"Lenox Hill Hospital . . ." Diana searched for the words: "My sister is having a baby today."

The taxi driver nodded as the car's clock ticked over: 4:23. Fifteen minutes to go.

"Alright we're—"

"Thank you, thank you," Diana muttered distractedly as she rushed out of the taxi.

"Hey, that's twelve dollars!" the taxi driver called after her as she swung open the hospital door.

Diana paused and winced, closing her eyes. She turned around and ran back to the taxi, slapping a few bills into the passenger seat before dashing back to the hospital doors.

"Hi, uhh, my sister, Diana Hung, is having her baby in—," Diana glanced up at the analog clock above the receptionist's desk, "three minutes—I mean um, h-her husband called and told me she was in labor." Diana winced. "Could you tell me her room number?" Diana finished, recovering.

"Sure, no problem." The receptionist smiled and began clicking around on her computer. "Looks like she's in room 213, just down that hallway."

Diana let out a sigh of relief. "Thank you," she breathed as she grabbed her visitor's pass.

She walked briskly down the familiar hallway and stopped abruptly. 213. Diana pressed her ear against the door, recognizing her own cries of pain. She thought she could hear the quiet, comforting voice of her husband, still supporting her even as she squeezed his hand for dear life. Leaning against the door, Diana closed her eyes wistfully, allowing a tear to run down her cheek.

Suddenly, she pushed away from the door and backed into the center of the hallway.

"What am I doing?" she whispered, "What did I think I was going to do? Steal Will?"

She slid her hand down her face. A cool sensation ran down her right forearm. Her gaze jerked down to the copper bracelet; she yanked it off and threw it to the floor. Diana leaned against the wall across from room 213, contemplating. She sighed, scooped up the chain lying on the tile, and held it firmly in both hands.

She laughed bitterly to herself, whispering, "I could never have changed anything, could I? Maybe I can still go back—or forward I should say—and try harder. For Will."

The bracelet remained static in Diana's hands as she delicately reclasped it around her wrist. "I wish to go back to the present." The bracelet and the sky turned clockwise. Day and night blurred again, until it settled on day and gravity regained control of the bracelet.

Will paced in circles around the park bench, wondering how he would get back to where he was supposed to be. He stopped. If the bracelet had taken him here, it could take him back. He racked his brain trying to think of what activated the bracelet. But hunger interrupted his thoughts.

Will's stomach rumbled. He hadn't eaten in several hours since starting his essay—or should he say in two years? Will collected himself and took in his surroundings, recognizing he was just a few blocks away from his favorite pizza place.

As he walked along the still-crowded sidewalks, he solidified his plan to get back to where—or when—

he was supposed to be. He replayed his sudden time jump over and over again in his mind. The question consumed him: what had activated the bracelet? A pang of hunger snapped him out of it as the aroma of the pizzeria greeted him.

Moving toward the counter, he rustled through his jean pockets for loose cash. He came up empty handed. "Dang it," he muttered. He started to walk away when someone oddly familiar caught his eye. The guy ordered two slices of pepperoni pizza. Will spotted a copper glimmer on his wrist. *Huh. That's what I always order, and that looks just like my copper bracelet,* Will thought to himself. *Funny coincidence.*

He started to walk away from the pizzeria, but before he could, the pepperoni pizza guy (who Will had affectionately named his doppelgänger) laughed at something the shop owner told him. *Huh. I know that laugh too. Don't know where from, though …* The gears turned in his brain as he tried to place the laugh. Suddenly he stopped, turned, and stared at the pepperoni pizza guy. *Wait … that's my laugh.*

Instinctively, he hid behind the decorative trees outside the shop to avoid being seen by future him. Carefully, he peeked out from behind the tree and watched future him trip over the leg of a stray chair, causing his pizza to fall to the floor. Will winced and closed his eyes, bracing himself for what he knew would happen. But the yelling and cursing never came.

His clone's friends were bent over laughing, but future Will just smiled.

Will watched in a combination of confusion and amazement as future him calmly walked up to the counter and paid for another couple slices of pizza. He sat down with his friends, musing. "You don't even want to know how I would've reacted a couple years back. Let's just say that chair's feelings might've been hurt." Future Will took a bite of pizza. "But I guess I learned getting frustrated over everything's not worth it. There were a lot of things to get frustrated over a couple years back. It just would've been constant frustration if I kept tuning in to every little thing."

"Two years back," Will whispered, retreating back behind the tree. "2020 … the pandemic?"

He walked onto the crowded sidewalks and fidgeted with his bracelet. "I have to go back to my present," he whispered. Suddenly, something clicked in his brain: *A wish!* he thought. *That's how I got here.* He leapt up in excitement. Drawing in a deep breath, he whispered, "I wish to go back to my present." The bracelet spun around his wrist, clockwise this time. Faster and faster the days and nights rewound until they blurred into one and finally stopped.

Standing on the tiled floors of his kitchen, Will glanced up. Meeting his gaze, Diana stood by the old wooden chair pulled out from the kitchen table, as if she were waiting for him. Smiles of relief, acceptance, and joy spread across their faces, and they stumbled forward to embrace each other. No time like the present.

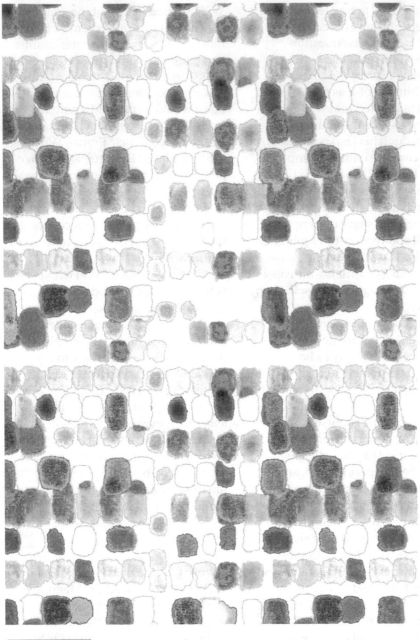

Waterdrop (Watercolor)
Ashley Jun, 13
Short Hills, NJ

The Read Aloud

When the writer struggled with reading, it seemed like everyone was willing to help her improve except her teacher

By Sophia Hammond, 11
New York, NY

There I was, sitting in my second-grade classroom in the School of the Blessed Sacrament. I was in the front of the room, crisscross applesauce on the yellow square of the rainbow rug—my favorite color. I was holding my *Charlotte's Web* book. I heard one of my classmates read aloud. I was silently wishing I was the one reading. I looked around the room and saw my tiny gray desk with my pink pencil case on top. Yellow was rather close to the teacher, so I could smell my teacher's lemon perfume.

My teacher's name was Mrs. Romeo. Mrs. Romeo had long brown hair and brown eyes. She was obsessed with her cat, Obby, and would talk about him every day. She had pearly white teeth and always had a big smile on her face, but she had favorites. I was not one of them, but she liked me.

This was one of my worst years at Blessed Sacrament. It was not that I did not have any friends, or that I got bullied. It was because I felt excluded from our class read-aloud. In second grade, I was not a great reader. I struggled to read chapter books.

When I was in kindergarten, I was the first one in my class to read 100 books. That was a big achievement for me. In kindergarten, I felt I was the best reader in my class. *Why did it go downhill from there?* I wondered.

It all started that day my teacher said that we were going to read *Charlotte's Web*. We all gathered up on the rug and my teacher gave out parts. I put my hand up, desperate to be chosen for a part. A couple days later, I was finally chosen. *Yes,* I thought. I stood up in front of the class.

I fumbled, "T-h-a-t is w-why you wi-will ne-n-nev-nev—"

"Never," Mrs. Romeo interrupted.

I stuttered on every part, and my teacher had to help on almost every word.

Why can't I be like my classmates? I thought. *I wish I could read like them.*

Because I stuttered on every word, I was not chosen again for a long time. And when I was chosen, I still stuttered. Even if I tried my hardest, I had to get help from Mrs. Romeo or another classmate.

My classmates helped me when I could not read a word. When I would read and I got stuck, they would call out the word and I would keep reading. I liked how my classmates would help even if I did not know them as well as others. My parents were also extremely supportive. They knew that the book was way above my reading level and above some of my other classmates' too. They tried to find a way to help me improve my reading skills. My mom tried to read out loud with me, but I preferred reading in my head. The only person who did not seem to help with this situation was Mrs. Romeo. She would not try to improve my reading. Mrs Romeo did not seem to help me in any way.

At lunch one day, I was sitting with my friends Colleen and Danielle. We were talking about Play-Doh. Then I said, "Do you notice that I don't get picked to read aloud at all?"

"Yes," they both said. "Jinx."

The boys overheard this conversation, and J.P. said, "She also yells at me for asking someone to help me, but all the girls are helping each other."

"I did notice that, but why?" I said, a little confused. It was a comforting thought to know that I was not the only one that did not like the way the teacher treated my classmates and me.

When I was reading I felt embarrassed, and I thought this changed the way people thought of me. I thought I was the worst reader in the world.

For the rest of second grade, my parents came up with a plan. We got a tutor after school. I was mad at my parents at first because I thought it was weird and that people would laugh at me. But then I realized that my tutor was seeing me at home so no one would know about her. I also took a test at the Department of Education to try and find out why I was struggling with reading. It was a long test and it seemed weird. After the test, I went back to school and people asked where I had been. I wanted to keep it a secret, so I said nothing. When we finally got the test results back from the Department of Education over the summer, we realized I needed extra help at school too.

When third grade started, I felt scared because people would find out I had a tutor. I didn't want people to know I had a tutor because they might think I was dumb. During school, I had to leave the room to work with the tutor. I had to take tests in another classroom and go to her after school. I felt different and frustrated because everyone knew I needed help.

Turns out, it was one of the best things that has happened in my life so far. My tutor's name was Ms. Susan. She had curly blonde hair and glasses. She made me feel joyful. She made the lessons fun and gave me treats. Also, I did not feel alone because I worked with two other boys who struggled with reading and spelling. I worked on my reading skills over the next couple years to get on the same reading level as everyone else.

After all of this hard work, it finally paid off. I am now able to read chapter books at grade level! I also realized that no one cares how well you read. They care about how you treat them and others. Also, that everyone struggles with something and you are not alone. I feel I have improved a lot the past couple of years, but there is still much more to learn.

Two Weavers (iPhone, Procreate)
Madeline Cleveland, 11
Belleville, WI

Northern Lights

By Raeha Khazanchi, 11
Rochester, NY

When those northern lights shine
Spewing out rainbows
To color the snow.
When purple and blue dances with my hair,
Turning it purple then blue then purple again
Until it settles for a violet blue the color of blueberries.
When the snow turns green
And my house, black,
We all know that the sky has turned on
A private play
That only we get to see.

Waterfall

By Jillian Carmel, 9
Denver, CO

Crashing to the ground
So silent but very loud
It's nature's magic

Highlights from Stonesoup.com

From the section of our blog devoted to writing inspired by COVID-19

Life Now
A digital artwork

By Mika Sarkar Omachi, 12
San Francisco, CA

Artist's Note:

This digital art is a human-shaped fishbowl. Fishbowls are like a cage because the fish can't go anywhere, but they also protect the fish by keeping them in water. This is like shelter-in-place because we are all separated from each other, but also we are always at home where we can be observed like fish in a fishbowl.

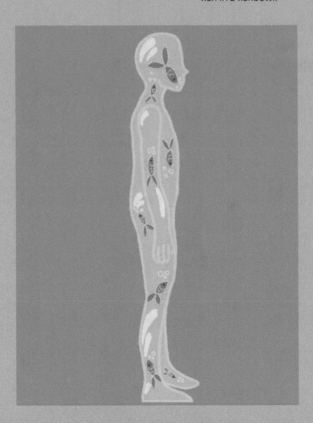

About the Stone Soup Blog

We publish original work—writing, art, book reviews, and multimedia projects—by young people on the Stone Soup Blog. When the pandemic began, we got so much incredible writing about the experience of living through the lockdowns that we created a special category for it! You can read more posts by young bloggers, and find out more about submitting a blog post, here: https://stonesoup.com/stone-soup-blog/.

Honor Roll

Welcome to the Stone Soup Honor Roll. Every month, we receive submissions from hundreds of kids from around the world. Unfortunately, we don't have space to publish all the great work we receive. We want to commend some of these talented writers and artists and encourage them to keep creating.

ART

Ella Bushaw, 10
Nyla Kurapati, 8
Ava Shorten, 11
Jiacheng Yu, 6

PERSONAL NARRATIVES

Ava Anderson, 11
Stephen Eidson, 13
Teresa He, 11
Keira Huang, 11

PLAYS

Mussharat Prottoyee, 8

POETRY

Harper Clark, 10
William Grammatis Cooke, 13
Harper Eves, 8
Maya Mourshed, 9
Eric Muller, 10
Aishwarya Vemulakonda, 9
Leilani Wurdak, 8

STORIES

Michaela Frey, 13
Violet Galati, 8
Zola Gargano, 13
Apoorv Gupta, 12
Hiyaa Kashyap, 10
Olivia Lee, 10
Aaria Nair, 13
Graham Oakey, 11
Ilsa Peterson, 12
Taylor Rooney, 8
Isaac Weng, 13

CPSIA information can be obtained
at www.ICGtesting.com
Printed in the USA
BVHW051957041021
618108BV00001B/2